THE TRIAL OF SATAN

A CONFRONTATION BETWEEN MEN AND THE
NUMBER ONE PUBLIC ENEMY

Jemadari Vi-Bee-Kil Kilele

Order this book online at www.trafford.com
or email orders@trafford.com

Most Trafford titles are also available at major online book retailers.

Frontispiece: Prince Mundeke

Printed in the United States of America.

ISBN: 978-1-4269-4387-4 (sc)

Library of Congress Control Number: 2010913792

*Our mission is to efficiently provide the world's finest, most comprehensive book publishing
service, enabling every author to experience success. To find out how to publish your
book, your way, and have it available worldwide, visit us online at www.trafford.com*

Trafford rev. 10/04/2010

 www.trafford.com

North America & international
toll-free: 1 888 232 4444 (USA & Canada)
phone: 250 383 6864 ♦ fax: 812 355 4082

Contents

The Trial of Satan; by Prince Mundeke, 2004

For **Don Montezuma Kaluseko**,

In frank remembrance of long standing friendship and our divergent believes.

If the Devil was that bad, and if he was created by God, the same God would not have allowed him to live that long and perform all the evils he's been so far accused of.

J.V.B.Kilele

List of Characters

1. The crowd in the street
2. The urchin/street kid
3. An old man and his wife (Thando)
4. Two persons from the crowd in the street
5. A (boy) newspaper vendor
6. A woman buying newspaper
7. A drunkard person
8. The Court Presenter [CP]
9. The Judge President [J.P]
10. First Assessor [F.A]
11. The Public Prosecutor [P.P who is also a priest]
12. The Second Assessor (S.A)
13. Satan
14. Two advocates (1 & 2) from the audience
15. Three intervening persons from the audience (A, B & C)
16. A policeman guarding Satan
17. Four policemen ensuring security in the court
18. The court audience in general [±15 persons]
19. Strange characters

ACT 1: SCENE 1

[In a street of a country named Dunia Yetu, on planet earth, an urchin is hailing passers-by and bystanders in broken English. Street vendors are bustling about their businesses. He goes up the street, shouting through a megaphone, distributing flyers to the amazed crowd. Some people are picking up falling pamphlets and start reading them and chatting to one another]

The urchin:
All, to de court, to de court. A big event today, a big one, ladies and gentlemen! To court to hear human justice making history. Le'go, le' all go to de court!

The crowd:
What! Hein, what's happening? What are you talking about?

The urchin:
De devil, de devil. De earth police arrested Satan during a routine patrol and have taken him to court for judgment.

An old man in the crowd:
Goodness me! *[Talking to his wife]*: Thando, Thando.

Thando:
My love.

The same old man:
Listen to what this hobo's saying.

Thando:
What is he saying, lovy?

The same old man:
That the devil has been apprehended by the patrol of planet earth police.
Thando:
It sounds serious but also amusing. Sweetie, please, approach him a bit in order to re-confirm this matter, my dear.

Someone from the crowd (1):
It's a classified piece of information. Take it seriously.

Another person from the crowd (2):
Don't give it a damn credit now. You've got to check it out before you believe in all these city gossips of which people are sick and tired. It's just unbearable.

A woman coming to buy a newspaper:
Oh! Yeah! Their headlines are always enticing. One can't resist buying newspapers. [*To the street vendor*] What's on the news today, my boy?

Newspaper Vendor:
The devil, Satan's been arrested since yesterday. Read this headline.

Same woman: (*Holding the newspaper and reading it*)
What? My God! Is this possible?

Another person in the crowd (1):
[*Speaking to the lady*]: Yeah! The devil. Ask my boy here. He's seen him.

Same woman:
Are you serious? Seen him? With his eyes?

Another person in the crowd (1):
In flesh and bone. I tell you what. My boy, [*to the urchin*]. What's taking place? How does he look like?

The urchin:
Who, Satan? He's been hand-cuffed. Over there, over there… He is an ugly character, with horns above his head, long nails and most disgusting of all are his sharpened and long teeth.

Same woman:
Don't tell me! Are you kidding? The devil! You mean Satan? Hein!

The urchin:
To court, to court, let's all go to court. He's been arrested and is appearing in court today.

A drunkard man from the crowd:
[*Holding a bottle of beer and limping*]: Who? Who's gonna arrest me? Who prevents you from taking beer? You have no money. Go away with your comedy. [*(pushing the boy away)*]; poor, all of you poor men. Clear my way, you bunch of jealous people.

The same old man:
Don't torture him. He's not crazy, though famished. Listen to what he's saying first. Hein! Don't be so bullish towards him. The little boy's claiming Satan's been arrested, my dear… We've got to go and watch what's gonna happen out there.

3

The drunkard:
You too are talking shit; move away, and far you go from my sight. Naïve vermins [*pushing him away. Then he falls down*]

Thando:
[*Beating the drunkard man with her hand bag*]: Stop this war here, stop it. Hold my hand lovey [*leaning on her husband.*]

The same old man:
I will get you next time. Vengeance is a dish that one eats coldly. [*Standing up*]

The drunkard:
Next time. Oh yes! I don't pass here every time.

Thando:
Go away [*to the drunkard man*]. What were you talking about, boy?

The urchin:
… and now, he is put on trial by human justice. [*all amazed*]

The same old man:
Listen to that! [*To his wife*]. He's gonna dance to our music.

The crowd:
The devil! Satan! Let's go to court, to court, magistrate court, high court [*They all rush, some falling on their way, other fighting to be the first to go*]. Wait for me, … I must see him today …, the devil, Satan … Help me…

[*Media reportage cars, journalists, photographers, cameramen rush to the scene*]

ACT 1: SCENE 2

[A moment later, people are thronging inside the court house. The media are there. People chat and are curious. Then the jury enters after the Court Presenter has addressed the audience]

Court Presenter:

Respectable audience, the Devil has just been arrested under the allegation of misleading the whole humanity, the mankind. But, we don't know, august audience, how he should be prosecuted. Ladies and gentlemen, in the history of man's justice, it is a strange case. To expedite this matter, prior to an international Court of Justice, a special tribunal has been set up, essentially composed of a Religious Minister who acts as the Public Prosecutor, of a Magistrate who acts as the Judge President, of a Police Officer who stands in as First Assessor and with an army officer as Second Assessor. The Devil is accused of misleading people to do evil. Dear president and respectable audience, since the word "evil" sounds like "devil", at this stage, nobody may yet predict what will be the outcome of this case.

Court Presenter:

Court rise!

[The hall stands up and noise ensues]

[*Enter the hall, Advocates, Judge President. The audience is still standing up*]

Court Presenter:
Thank you. [*The audience sits down. He drops a file on the Judge President's table, and then stands aside. Noise rises up from the crowd*]

Judge President:
[*Hammering the table*]: Silence! in court. The court is open. [*He reads the opening indictment sentence*]. This court of exception, giving a ruling on this day on the matter of mankind accusing Satan, invites the accused, Mr. Satan, to come forward to the dock and respond to the allegations leveled upon him.

Second Assessor:
Accused, Mr. Satan, come forth to the dock. [*Satan advances. He is chained around the waist and* escorted *by a police officer to whom the chain is attached too.*]

Policeman:
[*Speaking ironically and apologetically to the Judge President while untying his chain around Satan*]: My lord, I had no other option. For, nobody knows what would happen had he escaped. It was a precautionary measure. You know how many centuries it has taken us, human beings, to get hold of this crafty character. We have suffered a lot since creation up to today. Fortunately, the mighty God does not sleep. And today, we've got this chap.

Judge President:
Why is he manacled like that? Does he feel comfortable?

Second Assessor:
I am sorry; I had to do this to guarantee his custody for the sake of justice. [*Pause. Then he unchains him*]

Judge President:
Thank you, officer. Accused, do you acknowledge to be Satan, the devil and the father of all evils, according to the Holy Bible?

Satan:
Look, look, [*nodding*] once more, that is another blunder; because, I am not the devil. I am not Satan. In order to please your pretension, I allowed you to arrest me. Straight from that time, I told you that I was not Satan. That, my real name is Lucifer.

Judge President:
Accused, Mr. Lucifer; do you still maintain your first statement that, during all this trial you won't need an advocate to ensure your defense?

Satan:
Your honour, I maintain my statement. Nobody can take my defense; because nobody knows me much better than I do. Besides, my extreme intelligence will preside over my destiny. I am not as easy as you presume.

Judge President:
Accused, Mr. Satan; would you please be more explicit on this very point?

Satan:
Your Honour; dear advocates and dear audience too, we are all God's creatures. You, like me. But me, Lucifer that you wrongly call Satan; I am more intelligent than human beings are. How could it then be possible that you, human beings, could take the defense of a creature which is above your intelligence? That clearly proves that you are narrow-minded, that you have a mind which is purely corrupt, that you have corrupt your judicial apparatus with saucy words and ambiguous systems which can only be

interpreted by an adventurer who was initially trained by a liar in a school of lies; and you call such an adventurer, an advocate, a lawyer, a public prosecutor, an attorney or a magistrate.

First Assessor:
[*Standing up*] Don't exaggerate!

Satan:
I don't. It's none of my intentions. Now, Mr. President and respectable audience; what in fact is a lawyer? A lawyer is a vulgar impostor, a liar. How can't we talk about lie when the truth is that the court always pretends to look for the real culprit, yet the lawyer knows him or her very well? Dear President and respectable audience; I intentionally say that the court pretends to look for the guilty person, while in reality, the court perfectly knows that lawyers are aware of all the truth, but they indulge in buying time! Then, why can't you compel lawyers to give statement for the sake of justice, in the name of the law? And, in case he refuses to give evidence, he should be prosecuted for obstruction to the course of justice.

An unexpected she-advocate from the attendance (1):
Objection my lord. I am sorry to intrude in this, but this avalanche of verbosity from this alien should be stopped right now. He is denigrating our profession and we can't allow this rubbish to go on unattended to. Something should be done, sir.

Judge President:
I concord; but let us listen to him. You never know what aliens may export to our world since our justice system is not the same. We may learn something from theirs. Understand that, globalization does not only concern planet earth. To some extent, it is somehow heading towards inter-planetarian globalization and expertise exchange. And, we lose nothing by exchanging views

in our field. Who knows, Mr. Satan can turn out to be a heavy weight consultant in our judiciary system. [*laughter*]

The same she-advocate (1):
What?

Judge President:
Madam, our legal system seems to be obsolete, and in order to adapt to new trends; we need to be lectured by an unscheduled visitor. Don't be obstructive, madam advocate, with all due respect to you, madam; let me tell you that big minds should talk to one another in order to produce light where darkness prevails.

The same she advocate (1):
Goodness me! Am I dreaming or what?

Judge President:
You are not, madam. Freedom of speech, freedom of thoughts, authoritative arguments have no room here, madam. If freedom was the essence of life, therefore every creature should enjoy it.

Satan:
Thank you Mr. President. You sound as if you have visited the heavens before I got harassed by these agents of your corrupt and old-fashioned justice system. Look how they are dressed, your lawyers! This is a colour of death, found on a hearse, dressed by mourners and bereaved people. Oh! Your lawyers are mentally dead long time ago.

The same she-advocate (1):
I'd better vacate the hall. A Court President? Condoning garbage from an illiterate and cunning mind! How come? This is a **grande première** in the history of law.

Judge President:
[*Hitting the desk with a hammer*]: Silence. Either you keep quiet or vacate the hall. [*He stands up, and angrily warns*] One more word, you will be banished from the legal corporation. One.

The same she-advocate (1):
I am sorry, my lord [*She sits down*].

Judge President:
Mr. Satan, Please, carry on.

Satan:
Remember, I am not Satan. Nonetheless, thanks for the support, Mr. President.

Judge President:
I am not supporting you; I am just speaking on behalf of the Law. On this planet, the court is always impartial. The court is here to hear what people say and guide their interventions in order to avoid deviation of human emotions. We discourage extremisms and senseless radicalisms.

Satan:
The law is you and you are the law since it is crafted by you, sir. Anyway, I was just saying that when an accused person tries to defend himself, his opinion is already hijacked by his lawyer who is always in advance in all statements. So, the court will always tell you that, "owing to legal professional ethics, the lawyer is not allowed to expose all what his client has told him." On the other hand, they will tell you that "the lawyer cannot betray his client."

Judge President:
So, what? You mean, lawyers protect culprits?

Satan:
Well, that's another big mistake: "professional ethics, client, betrayal of the client he represents", etc. But, dear human beings, in which way do you plan to render justice to your world? How can you call a guilty person a client? What type of justice is that? Is it that, you are short of proper and exact vocabulary or what? I personally don't think so. Because we could also call the alleged culprit a patient, just as medical doctors call sick persons; because, be it for the alleged culprit or the real patient in the hospital, both are waiting for a verdict according to the law or a diagnosis from the medical report. But then, why not call each of them "patient"? Because both of them are in a dire need to be treated, to be attended to by someone who is supposedly an expert.

Second Assessor:
Objection, your Excellency. The truth is that...

Judge President:
Objection rejected. Let him continue. Justice should be impartial and non-partisan. Even if he does not look like us, we should apply the just law so that, if he has got the chance to go out of our sentence, he should return to wherever he comes from with good remembrance or our planet. Mr. Satan.

Satan:
Your Honour...

Judge President:
Please, keep it up.

Satan:
[*Smilling*] You are such a respectable authority. Even in heavens, you'll get your place if you remain uncorrupt as you are trying to prove so far.

Judge President:
Nobody knows. To see God, I must die first. Please, continue. Initially, I warned you to stop making such humoristic statements.

Satan:
Frankly speaking, dear human beings, it is that cupid mind, that endless money-grabbing attitude that pushes you to call a criminal a client. Dear advocates, if there are any in this hall; I want to state that, by qualifying your protégé as client, you unconsciously betray your hidden vow of commercializing the justice system. Because, in business, as I remember, there is a sacred principle stipulating that "the client is always the king"; and therefore he should be protected. So, all along the hearing session, you battle in order to win the trial, because you are fighting for your king, who has paid you in advance. Dear human beings, and you ignorant jailers, this is corruption of the justice system.

Someone from the audience (A):
We respect your deduction, but, that's how things are being done in here, sir. Accused people are always legally represented by their attorneys. Why should it be different from you? In Rome you must dance like Romans. It's as simple as that.

Satan:
What is Rome?

Someone from the audience (B):
It's a city in Italy.

Satan:
That city was destroyed long ago by the injustice of Emperor Nero. Long before you got born. I was there. And, now, it is the city of world Mafia. Another plague against humanity, which you should deal with; not me.

Someone from the audience (C):
You are lying, Mr. Satan.

Satan:
Can you explain to me why all lawyers get dressed 99% in black and 1% in white? Yet, commonly you were taught that, black symbolizes bad, wrong and lie. All the negative things; and the white stands for purity. It simply means that, lawyers are liars and only little from them is true.

Judge President:
I find your interpretation another piece of lie, Mr. Satan.

Satan:
Is it? Really? Coming back to you Messieurs advocates, the climax of all paradox is that, your ambiguous system of justice disturbs the will of the accused person as well as that of the complainants who fail to really air their opinions because as you, their advocates are interested in their money, you don't want to lose the trial. What is amazing is that, the audience sees only the lawyer who speaks, who complains and accuses, all on behalf of his so-called "client". But, dear audience, all the lawyer's skills, all his speech just helps cover and deviate truth, or to reduce the truth of the offence committed by the criminal. Alas! Here comes the legal irregularity that legalizes irregularity.

[*Silence, he looks left and right, then shouts*]

You, a bunch of corrupt businessmen, bandits, crooks, thieves, tricksters, that's all what you are. If you human beings were concerned about real justice, advocates, medical doctors and all those who are in the liberal profession would be employed by the state. Just as soldiers are. In that way, you would never auction yourselves to any one who has money; because in the new order of things, you only prostitute your profession to anyone who has money.

Someone from the audience (B):
Objection, your Honour. May we stop this devilish comedy in here? We came here to judge this man, not him judging us!

Judge President:
Objection rejected. Democracy means tolerance. Let's listen to him and learn something from him. Please, be patient. Carry on Mr. Satan.

Satan:
Thanks, your worship. Dear human beings; your system of justice belongs to some noisy and talkative lawyers who are gifted by God in order to speak and convince. Dear human beings, your legal system is a filthy commerce, which belongs to those who have the power to buy it. Please, do not soil me. Dirty people who enjoy money can't represent me. Because, the word justice means "just ice" that means an ice which is clean, transparent, spotless.

Judge President:

[*After whispering*]: That's well stated, Mr. Satan. You are free to assume your own-defense as you demanded upon your arrest..

[*curtains down*]

ACT 1: SCENE 3

Second Assessor:
[*Standing up*]: Now, cherished audience, we are reading the charge sheet.

Satan:
How dare you?

Second assessor:
Don't interfere. This is our job.

Satan:
Stop it. [*The Second Assessor is amazed*] I don't think that's necessary. I am informed about the facts and details concerning my charge. In fact, I appear today in front of human beings' High Court on charge of inciting human beings to doing wrong. Human beings accuse me of misleading populations of your rotten planet to do evil, and this accusation dates back centuries ago.

First Assessor:
That's perfect. The charge is well-known by all of us in here; and it's true. Now, defend yourself, Mr. Satan.

Satan:
Your worship, for my defense; I confirm that all those accusations are fruits of the imagination of a psychopath; I mean human

beings are mentally abnormal. Because, I know, your worship and the whole court, that no man on earth is capable of establishing my guilt without bias. I am a scapegoat, a rubbish dump wherein every irresponsible creature hurls his waste in order to avoid accountability for their acts.

First Assessor:
Sorry, Mr. Satan for all the allegations. But, let's listen to what the Public Prosecutor has to say.

Judge President:
 Mr. Public Prosecutor, you have the floor.

Public Prosecutor:
Thanks, my lord. Your honour, Messieurs Advocates and dear attendance. The evidence establishing Satan's guilt is the Bible. It is this Holy Bible in its wholeness. In the meantime, let us refer to these two biblical passages: [*he opens the Bible*] Roman 7: 14-17 and Ephesians 6: 10-13. With your permission, I would first of all like to start with Romans 7, verses 14 to 17 [*he reads out the passage to the court*]

"*We know that the law is spiritual; but I am unspiritual, sold as a slave to sin. I do not understand what I do. For what I want to do, I do not do, I agree that the law is good. As it is, it is no longer I myself who do it, but it is sin living in me.*"

End of quotation.

Your Honour, I strongly stress that the Bible teaches us that he is the father of all evils [*pointing at Satan*].

Satan:
Mr. President, respectable advocates; I would not prefer to continue this trial without exposing that, if man is able to do only what he

does not want, therefore man is a mental case. He is abnormal. And as long as you refer to that book, which you call "holy" through which my name appears on each page, for allegations that I am not responsible for, human beings are …

First Assessor:
Accused, Mr. Satan, the Devil, you do not have the floor to speak. Shut up! Continue Mr. Public Prosecutor.

Public Prosecutor:
Thanks you, dear audience. I was going to read the book of Ephesians 6. Verses 10 to 13. I quote [*then starts reading out the passage*]

"Finally, be strong in the Lord and in his mighty power. Put on the full armor of God so that you can take your stand against the devil's schemes. For our struggle is not against flesh and blood, but against the rulers, against the authorities, against the powers of the dark world and against the spiritual forces of evil in heavenly realms. Therefore put on the armor of God, so that when the day of evil comes, you may be able to stand your ground, after you have done everything, to stand.

Judge President:
So?

Public Prosecutor:
Your Honour, this is ultra important. The Bible stipulates that we are not fighting against men of flesh and blood, but against whom are we then fighting? Against who? Your Honour, this is what the Bible says: We fight against bad leaders who live in this world; like this devil spirit, and also battle against other evil spirits who reside in the invisible world. [*Holding out the Bible*]. The Bible is crystal clear on this very juncture; it tells us. [*Continuing with the reading*]"

"put on the armor of God, so that when the day of evil comes, you may be able to stand your ground, after you have done everything, to stand."

End of quotation.

Judge President:
That's fine.

Public prosecutor
My lord, the Bible adds on that, in all struggles, one must have faith as shield in order to resist against the enemy, against his spears and spurs. Your Honour, dear advocates and admirable audience. To cape it all, the Bible confirms that, in order to be able to face the diabolical ruse, we must hold up our faith. Accused Satan the Devil, these few passages must be sufficient for you to understand that your cheating is the cause of the two greatest world wars which have jeopardized the world around 1914 to 1918 and between 1940 to 1945. You were and still are the cause of wars in Biafra, Somalia, the Congos, Angola, Nicaragua, etc…

Satan:
Unbelievable [*pounding the ground*], unacceptable allegations, fabricated lies, unfounded evidence, Mr. President, I am afraid, human mind will never grow up.

Judge President:
Stop, accused Satan, you don't have the floor.

Satan:
I am sorry, Mr. President, understand my emotion against wrong accusations. This man is raving.

Judge President:
Continue, Mr. Public Prosecutor.

Public Prosecutor:
The cunningness of the Devil, say I, also ravages the humanity in endless wars in the Middle East, the Far East and the Near East. Should I continue to illustrate the damages that your evil mentality has caused in this world, I would talk about the apex of glory and power at which some mentally disturbed people have reached in this world. There have been criminal and racist individuals like Adolph Hitler, Pik Botha, Hendrick Vervoerd, who were acclaimed as great men, imperialistic defenders but who were a collective of thieves and assassins, racist, selective minds... . The likes of Mobutu Sese Seko, Nicolaeu Ceacescu, Jean Claude Duvalier and other dictators who tortured and terrorized innocent people across the world, to name but a few, all phenomena of absolute evil are consequences of the evil you have generated in the world. Deceiver.

Judge Prosecutor:
Enough, Mr. Prosecutor [*standing up*]. Accused Satan the Devil, you have the floor.

Satan:
Dear President, all what the Public Prosecutor has just said is totally wrong and more than false. Why don't you send for an ambulance and a medical doctor in order to treat him? He is sick. Dear Excellency, I have never enticed anybody to do wrong and have never provoked any phenomena of evil in your rotten world nor anywhere else. Gentlemen, I Lucifer whom you wrongly call the Devil, have great qualities that your stereotyped ideas and prejudiced reasoning towards me prevent you from appreciating. Dear human beings, there is in me a virtue that one can discern should one use a bit of good sense. That virtue is sincerity; besides, it is that which the salient feature of my character is. I am a sincere person.

First Assessor:
Accused Devil…

Satan:
Yes, Mr. Judge

First Assessor:
Concerning your sincerity as you pretend, would you like to be a little bit broad and explain to the audience in details, what is your sincerity all about?

Satan:
Certainly, Mr. President, advocates and respected audience. Your book of reference, the Bible teaches that all who do wrong have a common father: the Devil; because according to it, the Devil has never been a good person, the Devil has always been doing wrong. Isn't it? Dear creatures, starting from the hypothesis that, it is me the Devil that you keep on talking about, as you maintain it since the beginning of this comedy. Suppose that, I am really the Devil, we can conclude by that fact that I am the Devil, I have never been good and I always have been doing evil. I am therefore fundamentally bad. That is, in me there is no germ of goodness at all. Consequently, I am sincerely bad. Thus, sincerely I am pure in wrongdoing. Yet, all that is pure, dear human beings is genuine and in the basic notions of genuiness, one may detect the sincerity.

Second Assessor:
Satan, the accused, you seem to be extrapolating on this subject of your sincerity. Could you please be concise and precise?

Satan:
Gladly, let me explain this in very simple words, and maybe provide examples. Mr. Saul who later became apostle Paul was ill-treating Christians! He was severe with them. That, everyone allegedly

knows about it. But, his harshness, justly, was based on the fact that he had religious convictions; and, for your information; his deep religious conviction was Judaism. God has seen that in that man, there was a virtue, but because his virtue was badly directed, he was killing Christians. By that fact, God had converted him into Christianity, which is thus the real religion according to your book of reference, which is the Bible. The one you are carefully holding over there [*pointing at it*].

Another person among the audience (C)
Objection, Mr. President.

Judge President:
Yes, anything new? Please, come in.

Same person in the audience (C):
This guy is blaspheming and confusing anybody whose comprehension is below his malicious spirit. There is a lack of lucidity in his speech. Look, Christianity is not religion; besides it is a doctrine of belief. Because, religion is a set of methods invented by man in order to communicate with God and subjugate the humankind. But, belief is the medium used by God to reach man whom besides is caged in fanatical faith.

Judge President:
Thank you for the clarification. [*Smiling*] You know, I go to church but I never thought of what you have just said. It's marvelous. Mr. Satan the Devil, do you still have any arguments left?

Satan:
Certainly. Mr. President. It's still early to ask me such a silly question. To go back to what I was saying about Mr. Saul, who later became Paul, honorable audience, there was in that man a dose of virtue which was badly applied. In the same way, there are also cases where virtue is well-directed. But, it is other people,

those who observe… They are the ones who must change their opinion towards that virtue. What I want to say is that, if God is sincerely good and the Devil is sincerely bad, it just means both are sincere. But the problem rises only in the way their virtue is applied. Dear President, I want to conclude this argument by another example: the scholar who has invented the antibiotic drug called Penicillin and the other one who has invented the atomic bomb; aren't they both sincerely intelligent?

Judge President:
Of course, they are.

Satan:
Ah, you see? You see now? Thanks, honorable President. I like you for that.

Judge President:
[*Hammering the table*]: Mr. Satan, please, do not corrupt our mind. Please, continue. This court needs solid arguments for your defense, not destructive words.

Satan:
[*Smiling*]: Before the Judge President stopped me, I was questioning about the emanation of intelligence between a world healer and a world killer. I was talking about medicine and mass destruction weapons; I mean atomic bomb. Isn't it that both received sincere intelligence from the same God?

The audience:
Sure, they did!

Satan:
Now, if there is a person who does wrong and another one who does well, yet they are all inspired by the same God, whom will you blame? That person or God?

The audience:
God, of course. Oh! It is him, God, who is the originator of everything.

Public Prosecutor:
[*Rising from his seat and shouting at the audience*]: Stop it, stop it you squad of sinners. You are insulting the father of creation thanks to whom you are in this hall, thanks to who you exist, you breathe, and you speak. My father will delete you from this earth if you allow your belief to be corrupt by this incredulous bandit, whom, after receiving all the favors from God, betrayed him. Stop being influenced...

Satan:
You see. It is always the same narrow-minded species on this earth. Emotion always rules over reasoning.

Judge President:
[*Ironically*]: Dear Public Prosecutor, please, no emotion on earth as our visitor demands.

Public Prosecutor:
Accepted, your Excellency.

Judge Prosecutor:
Mr. Satan, please, proceed.

Satan:
It is rare to find reliable friends on earth like you, Mr. President [*laughter from the audience*]

Judge President:
[*Hammering the table*]: Stop it now. [*Then a long silence. He consults the rest of the jury, then, resumes*] Respectable audience and advocates, we are sorry to interrupt this hearing...

The audience:
Why, why? Why? But why? Hein?…

Judge President:
[*Keeps on hammering the table*]. Silence in the court, Silence. Owing to some administrative hiccups, we resume tomorrow at 09:00 sharp. [*Protest arises from the audience*]

[*Down curtains*]

ACT 2: SCENE 1

[At 09:00 a.m, the court hearing resumes next day, in the same hall. The audience is composed of the same attendance]

Judge President:
Yesterday, the accused, Mr. Satan ended up irritating the community of human beings as his cunningness was trying to corrupt our minds. However, according to his logic, he was trying to clarify his stand point on the question of the origin of intelligence and how creatures are free to use it. Mr. Satan, you have the floor.

Satan:
Thanks, Mr. President. I am complaining about one thing; that is, all night along, my privacy as a prisoner was not respected. All my movements were monitored, as if I were a sworn criminal. I have learned that there was democracy on earth, and being wrongly accused, there should be respect to some democratic...

Judge President:
Objection, Mr. Satan, you are in custody until your innocence is proven. And for security reasons, no bail will be granted to you. Mr. Satan, you have refused to be legally represented. Both your constitutional and individual rights are also fully guaranteed. So, please, do not ask for privileges. On our planet, prisoners receive equal treatment, sir. No matter whom you are. It's not a matter

of seniority or juniority, or else top ranking, but, it's equality in front of the law.

Satan:

[*After a pause*]: Well. Yesterday, I was asking: isn't that intelligence is a virtue? A proverb goes that "Science without moral is the destruction of the soul". In the two examples I gave yesterday, I meant that, the one who invented the medical product used his intelligence to improve the conditions of life on earth while the second, who invented the atomic bomb, used his intelligence to destroy the humanity. Briefly, even if you assert that I am wrong, I repeat that, with my sincerity, I am like a glittering gold in the hands of a poor man. I am not what you think I am. You are pressing a wrong button. You are mistaken about my identity. It seems, I am not the person you've been looking for ever since.

Judge President:

So, if we could understand, Mr. Satan the Devil, you mean, your sincerity is an acquired natural gift?

Satan:

Sure! Mr. President. Absolutely, it is.

Judge President:

Thus, we are the people who badly understand it and who misjudge you for nothing. Is it what you mean, Mr. Lucifer?

Satan:

Exactly, Mr. President. I am an innocent creature. I do the will of my sender. And, please, stop wasting my precious time.

Judge President:

Accused, Mr. Devil, sorry, Lucifer;

Satan:
Mr. President.

Judge President:
Are you capable of proving your sincerity? Your innocence?

Satan:
Mr. President, not long ago I was saying, your book of reference, the Bible, teaches that every evil-doer has for father the Devil. [*Long pause*] Mr. President, I am sorry, I seem not to be feeling well after all those night's tortures I was subjected to by my custodians. May I be excused for a while? In order to buy your trust, I urge you to be accompanied by one of your assistants behind the hall.

Public Prosecutor:
Pay attention Mr. President. He wants to run away.

Judge President:
Hein!

The Guarding policeman:
Not at all. I am here for that.

One person out of the audience (A):

[*Strange and bizarre characters enter the hall*]
What is this? [*As he sees a group of strange persons entering the hall. In the meantime, as Satan goes out, a group of other devils enter the hall shouting and beating the Judge President and the advocates. Demons switch off the light and cries of pain are heard out of the darkness.*]

[Curtains down]

ACT 2: SCENE 2

[Lights are set onto the stage. As Satan and his custodian return to the court, they witness a strange scene as they find the Judge President and the rest of the advocates complaining about pains.]

Guarding policeman:
What happened? *[Speaking from behind Satan at the door step]*

[a silent moment. The president and the advocates stare at the devil]

Second Assessor:
Just as you went out, strange creatures came in and beat us up in such a disorderly way. Then, they switched off the lights. Under such oblivion, we never remembered which direction they took.

First Assessor:
We have no remembrance of how they looked like or how they managed to enter here!

Second Assessor:
[Pointing at Satan]: It could be your people. The security around the building is lax. People enter with cellular phones here, guns and all dangerous arsenals that cause death. This Satan might have called his evil spirits in here in order to cause havoc.

Satan:

[*As he is entering*] Do I have people? I am a lonely creature. I have no brother, no wife, and no child. You should start stopping those allegations. [*He and the police officer enter the dock*].

Judge President:

It's nothing. Invaders have gone [*referring to the attack*]. Defendant Satan; earlier, before you be excused, you were elaborating on your sincerity. I mean your honesty. Can you prove it to this court?

Satan:

Yes, Mr. President. I first of all want to establish that I am not the one who goes around to look for people in a bid to mislead them. It is not me! The Bible, your divine book is pretty clear on that point. And, I urge you, on that juncture, to please check the book of James 1 14-15. You notice that, all what I say is evident. If your sensitivity permits me, may I read the passage for you, Sir? I would be pleased.

Public Prosecutor:

No, Mr. President. This creature is not spiritually clean. He should not be authorized to touch the holy book, lest, he desecrates it.

Satan:

Euh! Listen to that bullshit. Who gives you that audacity to speak to me in that way?

Judge President:

Accused, Satan, the Devil.

Satan:

Mr. President,

Judge President:

Don't worry. The second assessor will read it for you.

Satan:
All my thanks, Mr. President. [*Smiling*]. The public prosecutor hates the truth.

Second Assessor:
Let's read the Epistle of John to James 1: 13-15. *"When tempted, no one should say, "God is tempting me." For God cannot be tempted by evil, nor does he tempt anyone; but each one is tempted when, by his own evil desire, he is dragged away and enticed. Then, after desire has conceived, it gives birth to sin: and sin, when it is full-grown, gives birth to death."*

End of quotation

Satan:
You see? I hope dear audience that we have attentively followed everything. With clarity, the Bible says that everyone is tempted not by the devil, but by his own desire... It generates sins; and sin, having reached its climax causes death. Do you see now? You will realize up to now that I am innocent. You have the intelligence of God, and it is it that pushes you to do wrong. Not me. Consider me as a creature similar to you. I have never created anything in my life.

Public Prosecutor:
Honorable President, dear audience; Satan the Devil pretends that he does not tempt anybody; but in the book of Genesis, who is that one who went to tempt Eve to eat the fruit of the forbidden tree; I want to say the tree of good and evil? It's who?

Satan:
I am coming to that point, I am coming. Just give me a chance.

Judge President:
Honorable audience, dear advocates; I was stating that, I am not the one who goes out and look for people in order to mislead them

into mistakes. But, in order to flash back to the question of Eve, the girlfriend of Adam, I recognize that there also; they accused me of being responsible; only that, I would like to realize that, I didn't go into the garden of Eden by myself. Besides, it was not a garden! It was a wild bush, a real jungle. In which garden do you find wild animals? To my knowledge; in a garden, things are in order, not what was in Eden!

First Assessor:
Mr. Satan, please do not fall out of the scope of the trial. Tell us; who entered Eve's intimacy? Not you?

Satan:
Well, listen. I went through another person whose appearance I impersonated: the serpent. The Bible teaches in Genesis that; the serpent was craftier than any of the wild animals the Lord God had made in that "garden". Here, the Bible does not talk about intelligence but of cunningness. Dear human beings, let's agree on one another. What is cunningness? A virtue? No. A vice. That's cunningness. Notice then that, from the beginning, the serpent had already been a vicious character and it is since the beginning, the serpent had already been a vicious character and it is from that breaking of law where the mechanisms of law came. Because, you should know, dear human beings, that, for me to intervene in your lives, you should first of all allow me to do it through your mental weaknesses. That is why your Bible teaches that__let me quote:

"Do not allow the devil to tempt you. Resist him and he will run away from you".

End of quotation.

Judge President:
That's right.

31

Satan:
Mr. President, by saying that, in that incident of the Garden of Eden, I am not the only responsible. It is the snake and I only who acted in complicity. If the snake had not shown that defect in him, well, my spirit would never had been invited; and, obviously, the devil would be avoided. I never act by myself. Truly, I was used by the snake, and, I promise you, one day, I will ask for damages from him. I was just escorting him as he always lives lonely. You know very well that few creatures approach him…

Public Prosecutor:
Honorable President, dear advocates: Why should the evil irresistibly attract the devil to that extent? Why? Why can't he, at one time be attracted by goodness? This man is the father of all evils. Nobody else. I find him guilty for that reason. So far, he has not proved anything yet that can militate for his release. He is the one who pushes people to do wrong, thus, he should be hung.

Satan:
Objection, Mr. President [*angrily*], objection! I protest against lies and misjudgment. If really I was the father of all evils, it therefore means before I came to exist evil never existed. Where then has this idea of doing wrong come to be in me, yet we all know that God is the creator of everything? By asserting that it is me the cause of all evils, you consequently confirm that I am another creator. I am God. Therefore, respect and worship me right now. You can't oppose the same God that you are worshiping; and defending. [*a deep silence, then noise arouses in the court. Then Satan continues*] I have never created anything, because, I am myself another creature. And, for your information, a creature just has the capacity to invent or to procreate, but not to create. Certainly, perhaps I am the medium through which evil had entered the world. But I am holy. Because, while everyone is against me, God allows me to live and work.

Judge President:
And then, and then…

Satan:
And then, and then, I did not come to earth by myself. It is by the instruction of God that I descended on earth, after being comically chased from heavens. Read it in Revelations 12; 9:

"The great dragon was hurled down___that ancient serpent called the devil, or Satan, who leads the whole world astray. He was hurled to the earth, and his angels with him."

End of quotation.

Judge President:
Amazing!

Satan:
Then, why, why has God decided to send me down to the earth? Was it impossible for him to keep me in heavens, next to him; in order to arrange amicably our differences without involving human beings? Could you ask him what was the reason?

Second Assessor:
Accused, Satan the Devil, to set the point straight; the evil is neither a creation nor an invention. It is just a deviation from good to evil. And the inhabitants of the earth, I mean our planet, regard you as the epitome of all evils that exist. And if today, they have decided to arrest you, it is because they want to get rid of evil in order to improve their relationships with God. What's your opinion on such an "accusation", Mr. Satan?

Satan:
[*Smiling*] Exactly, Sir. And me, I am a creature made for that very purpose. All what I do is to improve and maintain good and amicable relationships with God; so does he on his side; because, we need one another. God does not hate me. Only he is hypocrite and refuses to reveal all about our partnership. There is a contract of which you don't know.

Judge President:
Accused, Satan, the Devil...

Satan:
Mr. President.

Judge President:
How is it possible, Mr. Satan? Because, in reality you were God's hunch man in heavens. You enjoyed all favors and he trusted you. How can you persuade us that he created you for evil purposes? [*The audience laughs*]

Satan:
Unfortunately, you don't understand, Mr. President. ***Pro tempore,*** you are forcing me to say things that I was avoiding to expose in public; because, they are top secrets in the dossier between me and God. Mr. President and respected audience, I lived in the heavens as the deputy of God. In my role of deputy, I was assigned to canvas for the worship of God. Let me tell you. It was not an easy task at all. Read your Bible. What does it say? Isn't it that, it says that ***"Your God is a jealous God"*** and that anyone working for him must only adore him?

A he lawyer from the audience:
And then, what happened?

Satan:
What happened is that, I also wanted to be worshipped. That is why there happened a terrible clash between me and him. To prove you that, I was part and parcel of the creation process, you should refer to the Bible in Genesis 1, Verse 26... God says: *"let's make man into our image"*. He says, *"our"*. He does not say *"his"*. The "our" is me and him. Thus, because I know all the secrets of the laboratory of creation, and I stood as a sort of opposition political party that defects from the mother board; because I didn't want his dictatorship and spiritual terrorism from a partner who hijacked my leadership. That is why we split. With the help of some sellouts that he calls angels, he plotted against me, overpowered me, and finally I was chased from heavens and purposively hurled down on your rotten planet to serve, still for his interests. But, at least, we still are equal. He rules in the sky, and, down here, it's me.

Second Assessor:
Please, halt for a while. All this seems to be getting out of my nerves. Don't you remember that in Genesis 1:27, the Bible says *"So God created man in his own image, in the image of God he created him, male and female, he created them."*

Judge President:
[*Angrily*] Let him continue. Do not disturb his inspiration. Things are coming out now from the enigma of creation.

Public Prosecutor:
No, Mr. President. This man is abnormal. He is crazy. He should be sent to jail straight away. And rot in there for good.

Judge President:
Our justice Mr. Prosecutor should be gentle, even to aliens. Impartiality will remain our motto, until justice and truth triumph over evil. Please, no emotion here. Compose yourself.

Public Prosecutor:
Thanks, Mr. President.

Judge President:
You are welcome [*to the Public Prosecutor*]. Mr. Satan, please, carry on.

Satan:
Thank you Sir. I was saying, God, used a hit squad under the commandment of angel Michael, who was our bodyguard and who was in charge of security. Unfortunately, one third of heavenly creatures who knew nothing about the deal rebelled also against God and followed me on earth; because, them too were badly treated by him.

Judge President:
This means that you really are the mastermind of the rebellion and the incarnation of evil. An indomitable and prodigal son!

Satan:
Dear human beings. The Second Assessor has just defined it recently by saying that, the evil is neither a creation less than an invention, so to say. Rather, it is an emanation of deviationism. In very simple terms, that means this: the evil is a by-product of the creation; and me by the fact of being the incarnation of that by-product which is the evil; I am also a derived product, which you wrongly call "Satan, the Devil". The same reasoning may mean *en-passant,* that, if you accept me, you will discover the original identity that I am: Lucifer, the Angel of light. It is here, dear human beings that I should reveal you something surprising, an arcane between me and God, who indeed is a bosom friend. [*Laughter*]

Someone from the audience (B):
What is it, then? What do you know, you villain impostor? Why are you so braggart?

Satan:
[*After a moment of silence*]: Listen, ladies and gentlemen. Listen to me. Very complicated situations have occurred in the heavens as I have partially attempted to explain to you. It is difficult for you as inferior creatures, from which truth has been hidden to understand the gist of those issues as long as they are not related to creatures living in your system of universe. Only master creators and to some extent, creatures of my species can comprehend them. I am not the only one to fail to make you understand those supra-universe notions. Even God himself experienced the same problem. That's why it is written in the Bible that "*To men what is revealed and to God what is hidden*". Check it out, poor men.

Public Prosecutor:
Honorable President, that is a pure escape [*angrily*]

Satan:
I am not intending to…

First Assessor:
Mr. Satan, you do not have the floor. Please, continue [*to the Public Prosecutor*]

Public Prosecutor:
Thanks. I was saying, he is trying to escape; because, mind you, this guy is a liar, a myth maniac and as I initially said, he is a special psychological case to be seriously dealt with. He is demented.

Judge President:
Oh yes, one man's intelligence is one man's madness. [*Laughter from the audience*] Please, continue, Mr. Prosecutor.

Public Prosecutor:
Your Honour, dear audience, the master creatures and heavenly manifestations that Mr. Satan is talking about are products of his own imagination. They are not real. He just wants to vindicate himself in our eyes. And, in order to beautify his lies; he is using biblical references that he has been quoting as alibi. He is strong in amnesia, not in understanding. He is a schizophrenic.

Satan:
Waoh! Human beings can lie! You are as blind as your faith. You people cherish surrendering the wholeness of your life to the horrifying control of someone you don't know. Who is God besides?

Public Prosecutor:
Our father.

Satan:
And who is your mother? His wife?

Public Prosecutor:
You are just a damn incredulous character.

Satan:
Of course I am; for I refuse to be controlled by a dictator; an invisible, a fictitious tyrant who keeps on grudges against every little thing I do and who fears to come out of his millennial hidey-hole.

Public Prosecutor:
Honorable president, basing ourselves on all likelihood, this is what is evident. Satan the Devil, after rebelling against God, our creator, has become a bitter character, a jealous one for being expelled from the paradise family. Rebellious, he refused to repent his sins. He then has sworn to only doing evil. Hence, the confusing thesis of sincerity by purity in evil that he is defending. [*Turning to Satan* now] Defendant, Satan the devil, your thesis of sincerity by purity in evil is just paradoxical and, so long, it hasn't helped you out at all. You have become a futility.

Satan:
Dear advocate, allow me to praise the public prosecutor. I notice that he too is a high spirit in a chaotic faith.

Judge President:
Defendant Satan.

Satan:
Mr. President.

Judge President:
We don't praise anybody in the courthouse. We say what we have to say and we keep quiet if we have nothing to say. Please, do not distract the court. Mr. Satan you have the floor.

Satan:
Pardon me Mr. President. But, I could not resist such momentum from the elation of my heart. Well, let me come back to your trial. I wanted to say that there is an iota of truth in what the public prosecutor said, except that he has skipped something. Angel of light that I was, and still am, I was saint. It is not me who has proclaimed my holiness but it is the Bible and God altogether who did. And, by being holy as such, I was exempted from all evil things. That is the thing I wanted to rectify, Sir.

[He keeps quiet. Then after, carries on]

Dear human beings, Lucifer, it is me. *[Beating his chest]* I was with God in all his privacies. The Bible confirms it; then, hold up your breath. One day in the greatest secrets, God has assigned me a mission to accomplish. This is what he told me:

"Lucifer, my dear friend, and he was caressing my shoulder. You always have been loyal to me. I know you as a sincere guy and able of firmness, he proceeded. I know, you can't betray me. Go on earth and continue only to do all what is wrong, all that is contrary to good. As you are skilled in convincing anyone, that will help me to select the best out of my human creatures. Because, I want to get a matured man, a staunch believer who will succeed me one day".

Public Prosecutor:
My God!

Satan:
Oh yes! It is truly your God. You said. Nobody else's.

Public Prosecutor:
What a heresy!

Satan: *[after a stare]:*
I then left the heavens and started my mission as assigned. Chasing me was just a scenario mounted by me and God in order to make it credible to other creatures. By accepting such a risky mission, which himself God could not fulfill, I am therefore more faithful to God than you, human beings are! Refer to the book of Job 2: 1-3 where Satan went with angels in front of the Lord to present themselves and probably report back. A task that human beings cannot fulfill. That is why one day you will be surprised to find me in heavens again, at the right hand side of your heavenly father,

if not amongst the saints! And when God dies, I automatically replace him. Because I have never been excommunicated nor fired from my second position in the celestial organization. It is only a temporal friction between me and him. Pretty soon, many of you who call themselves pastors, bishops, archbishops, prophets and popes will be jobless as there won't be anybody to lean on with your allegations; because, I am always the scapegoat of your sins and misconducts.

Public Prosecutor:
Your Honour, this is unbearable [*He takes off one side of his pair of shoes and hits the table*]. Really, astounding! And, me, I find it superfluous to continue with this trial. I guarantee you; we are dealing with a very serious mental case. The defendant is delirious, he is talking nonsense, he is blaspheming, and we also are blaspheming as we continue listening to his profanations. Honorable president, the Bible says the one who sits at the right hand side of God is Jesus Christ only, our Lord and Savior, not this intriguing creature to whom we have given a chance of tormenting us in this hall. [*Shedding tears*] Dear President and respected audience, God is love. In no case can he match with evil. Little does this Satan know that his days are here down numbered. The Bible is very clear on that point and it remains non-challengeable. Let's read the book of James 1-13.

"When tempted, no one should say, "God is tempting me." *For* God *cannot* be tempted by evil, nor does he tempt anyone."

End of quotation.

Judge President:
Oh yes, that is clear Mr. Prosecutor. And, where is the negative side in all what the defendant has just said?

Public Prosecutor:

Mr. President and respected audience, if we have to accept the declarations of the defendant Satan the Devil, it is questioning all the process of creation. It means our own existence. And that is a sin; a suicidal process. Rather, we should be grateful to God for having created us. He gave us eternal life. He suffered to design us like an engineer. Therefore, we should believe only; don't reason. Do not question God's deeds. He is spotless. [*He raises his hands*]

Satan:

Oh! He suffered? Who asked him to create you? Ignorant, frightened creatures. You are created mortals. Does life or your existence have meaning if you have to die? Me and God are eternal. Yet, he claims he made you into our image! Naïve, poor and mortal creatures. I pity you. Life is futile for you. Your God enjoys only being praised; but he does not work as hard as I do.

Public Prosecutor:

And Jesus of Nazareth? Oh, Jesus! Peace be upon him. [*He makes the praying sign of crucifixion*]. Where is his place in all this? His death, was it a useless sacrifice? The redemption, is it a divine comedy? No, honorable president, no. I propose that, the defendant withdraws all his allegations in block, lest he aggravates the situation for the proceedings in International High Court to deal with suspicious creatures. And, at this moment, whatever could be done by mistake, through all his statements should be considered as non-evident and dubious. At this stage, we should not rush into conclusion, Mr. President, dear audience. For, the law rejects all what is not provable for the benefit of the doubt!

Judge President:

That's true, Mr. Prosecutor. I totally agree with you. As you all know, we are here in search for the truth! Nothing else.

Satan:
Mr. President, dear advocates and the audience; suppose that my declarations are true, it is therefore evident that they will remain non-checkable as Mr. Public prosecutor has just made it clear. Thus, the doubt still persists. However, Mr. Public prosecutor, as the law rejects everything that is not verifiable on behalf of doubt and righteousness, in the same way, the same law acquits, as well, the accused on behalf of the doubt. Mr. Public prosecutor, on that point I think we all do agree.

Judge President:
Your Honour, [*to the Public Prosecutor*] to some extent, what he is saying makes sense.

Second Assessor:
To some extent yes, but not fully. He still has to convince this court of his innocence.

Satan:
In order to continue responding to the Public Prosecutor's low level of allegations, he has certified somewhere in his indictment pronouncement that God does not tempt anybody. Well, Mr. Prosecutor, I would like to make you realize on that very point that your assertions are awfully wrong and baseless. Because, not only God tempts people, but he misleads them all the time. He is not reliable. Your worship; if God does not really tempt anybody as you strongly confirm it, how do you explain that the same God asks Abraham to offer him as a sacrifice his only son, Isaac? Mr. President, dear advocates and audience; isn't it that a temptation? How do you call such a deed?

Public Prosecutor:
No, honorable president, no, no, no, no and no! It is important to know that, it just was a trial; yes, God's trial in order to gauge the faith of Abraham. Trials are there to strengthen us while

temptations make us fail in front of the father of creation. Do you see the light now, Mr. Satan? Do you see the difference? You even had tempted Jesus Christ, our Lord, by bringing him on top of a cliffy mountain, proposed him all riches of the world; fortunately, he chased you away. You failed.

Second Assessor:
You are on the right track, Mr. Prosecutor. However, as we are not here to preach, one should control one's words. We well-know that you are a self-appointed minister of God and at the same time a qualified lawyer. We are afraid that, one side of yours is easily getting carried away by a talkativeness syndrome. Understand that the venues are not the same today. This is not a church. Please, avoid too much surges in your speech, sir.

Public Prosecutor:
Thanks, your worship.
[*To the defendant*]: You failed. Sure, you dismally did fail!

Satan:
Yes, I know that; but still I was doing my job. The world belongs to me. It was given to me by God as a compensation for expropriating my leadership status in heavens. And, you don't know what happened later in Jesus being crucified?

Public Prosecutor:
Jesus's crucifixion saved us from sins and we remain victorious thanks to his blood that he shed on the cross. You are nothing in front of our Lord. Nothing at all.

Satan:
Hein! Ask him why can't he kill me if I am nothing? Baby, I can see; you are not well-informed.

Judge President:
My God, what a courage! [*Holding his head*]. Carry on, Mr. Prosecutor.

Public Prosecutor:
Thanks, your worship. I was saying, when God tries us, he respects the boundaries of our forces. That is, when he realizes our weaknesses, he puts an end to his trials. Well, it is the case with Abraham. When Abraham was on the brink of slaying his only son, he was stopped by God. Thereby, God has been persuaded that Abraham was entirely committed to him. But, but, when, you Satan the Devil try us, you have another hidden agenda. Your goal has always been to misleading us beyond our boundaries up until we flounder in the muddy land of sins. That's where your method of trial becomes a temptation.

Satan:
[*Furious*] Sir, I protest, I protest and categorically reject once more in block all your groundless allegations. It is useless to pretend to bring to books a soldier under the allegation that he has committed murder during war time if those murders are not regarded as war crimes under the instructions of military hierarchy. The same way, you, you have no right to prosecute me; because, like a soldier sent on a mission, I am at the war front, and I am serving God. I, whom you are prosecuting at this moment, I do wrong, it's true; but still I remain an excellent person. Do you think, it is easy to manage a controversial life of being good and at the same time doing bad? Let me tell you; it is heartbreaking, it is daily torture, a perpetual torment; because an angel is a creature made to only doing good. But me, being a spy, I play double role! [*A long pause*] Faith espionage.

A she-advocate out of the audience (1):
Do you realize now that you are a hypocrite, a rebellious character who was designed to doing good and today has fallen in a sinning

bottomless pit? You have no chance to come out of this trial. The legal system that you are criticizing will convict you severely. You'll be nailed, Mr. Satan.

Satan:

But, daughter of Eve; why? Why me? You fail to prosecute the Holy spirit, the first creature to have raped an engaged and virgin woman and you turn on to me? Why is your legal system protecting a convicted criminal like Mr. The Holy Ghost who bedded Mary? Apart from me, he is the second angel to be sent on mission for His Majesty God. But, he missed his goal and failed prey to carnal desires of a weak woman, who indeed was asleep. But me, I am doing my job pretty well. [*The whole hall is amazed.*]

Someone from the audience (C):

Blasphemy, blasphemy, infamy on you. Heresy, heresy. Ignorant, ignorant; that what you are. Mary was never married at that time. She was a fiancée to Joseph.

Satan:

Nonsense. Garbage. Can you accept that someone sleeps with your girlfriend without her consent?

Someone from the audience (C):

Nothing is impossible from the father of creation. Everything belongs to him.

Satan:

Your court should as well prosecute that man called Holy Ghost for having failed to pay maintenance fees for raising Jesus-Christ. How holy can he continue to be while he is an irresponsible person who neglected his fatherly duties?

Someone from the audience (C):
The conception and birth of our Lord were an immaculate one and has nothing related to all your mundane nonsense.

Satan:
Biologically, that is nightmarish.

Someone from the audience (C):
Indeed, your opinion is not needed here.

Satan: [*after starring at him*]
Well, coming back to Jesus Christ, your Lord; you know very well that he died. Both you and I are accused by God and some naïve men of your kind, that we killed him. Yet it was a filicide. That's another scandal in the history of the humanity! How can you and I be accused of killing this poor guy, yet his own father, right from the beginning, created him to die? Biologically, your Jesus was a still born child in order to redeem you from sins as his father pretends. He was doomed. I mean, God, according to his logics, could not pardon you without sacrificing his so-called son! Which means Jesus' death was a divine ritual because nothing can be obtained from God without a bloody sacrifice. Well, he is an insatiable cannibal. And, who knows, what wrong have you really done which he could not safewaive himself! Why should God keep grudge against you up until now? Hein!

Someone from the audience (B):
It's mystery. Yes, mystery. Evil mentality like yours cannot comprehend the magnitude of divine mysticism. You need to abandon sin first of all before any ray of light falls on you. Get born again. Spiritually you are dirty. Blind.

[*Satan looks at him and nods*]

Public Prosecutor:
[*To Satan*]
Stop it, just stop it there you stupid.

Judge President:
[*to B-someone*] Carry on.

Satan:
[*Having not paid attention to who should take the floor,*] Now, because Jesus could not commit a suicide or else God himself could not publicly kill his son, God used a hidden hand; me, in order to carry out the deed. I went through the Rome and Jewish leaders of that time who wanted power and glory; I hardened their souls and hearts so that they could not release Jesus from condemnation, until he was killed.

Judge President:
And then,

Satan:
I still can remember, when I was piercing his hands to the cross, the poor guy was screaming, *"Eli, Eli, Lama sabachani?"* To say, "Father, father why have you abandoned me? It shows that he was not a God. Since when a God screams like that? It's just funny. Today, both you and I are guilty of killing Jesus Christ; yet it is God himself who killed his son! [*pause*] Because he gave the instruction. Therefore, how can we be held responsible for such a premeditated act? Also, the son accepted to die in order to please the father. So, why should you accept divine calumny?

[*Pause, there are rumours among the audience*]

But, the sins he seemingly died for are still there. Consequently, Jesus's mission on earth is an outright failure! A waste and a divine farce! Because, it seems, Jesus ended up rising up from the deads. Which means he never died? He was just sleeping.

[*A burst of protestation arises from the hall. People protest by throwing books and other items on to the devil. Police come in to silence them. Finally, the court president will declare the hearing close for that day.*]

Judge President:
[*Hammering the table*]: Silence, silence in the court. Silence. [*After a moment*]: Defendant Satan, on behalf of the court, I dare convey our apologies to you.

Satan:
[*After starring at him*] Thanks Mr. President. Emotion is the first stage of human's downfall. It is difficult to control your impulse, you know. Reason why you quickly die. You are too much of an impulsive nature; you human beings.

Judge President:
Ladies and gentlemen, owing to this unpleasant event, I declare this court closed again for today. The court resumes its hearing tomorrow morning at the usual time.[*he stands up*]

ACT 2: SCENE 3

[As usual, the president enters the court the last. Everyone stands up]

Judge President:
Ladies and gentlemen, this court is now in session again, and I am inviting the offended defendant, Mr. Satan, sorry Mr. Devil, oh my God, Mr. Lucifer to continue with his defense. Once more, I urge the audience to be tolerant and give chance to the suspect in order for him to exhaust all his arguments. Let not our emotion be a hindrance to the process of justice and democracy. It goes with human kind's reputation and dignity; you should know that we must market the image of our planet to tourists. Mr. Lucifer, you have the floor.

Satan:
Thanks Mr. President. I rectify that I am not a visitor on earth, but you are. Look, I rule the world. Like it or not. You keep on dying, leaving me always here, generation from generation. You know that pretty well.

Public Prosecutor:
So what?

Satan:
Dear human beings, once more, let us be serious. I dare tell you that, you are weak and lazy creatures. All of you. It suffices one

minute for you, if you fail in whatever thing you were doing to find you kneeling down, praying and making endless confessions in the void. You pray a God that you don't know and will never know. You will notice that, I never come together with men who endeavor to be righteous in front of God. Truly speaking, there are times I disturb their lives. But, one will ask me why? Why? Why don't I mingle with those so-called good people you meet and know? It is simply because I am not allowed to mix with them; and I have neither the right nor the power to interfere in their lives. Frankly speaking, I am not interested in them. So-called good people are in minority while the wrong ones are the majority. If democracy is the rule of the majority and a system blessed by God, in complicity with you human beings, therefore I am a democrat! A spotless and blessed man! That's why I have the world. Unlike under God's empire, where only few are chosen, my government has no restrictions in what you do. Reason why the majority is with me.

[A burst of laughter comes from the audience. Then a sudden silence]

Public Prosecutor:
You see, you see *[to the audience]*, you see, that's what I was talking about. Alas! Now he is admitting the guilt *[rumors in the court]*

Judge President:
[Hammering the table] Once more I say no emotion. Let him carry on. Mr. Satan you have the floor.

Satan:
Honorable President, all my respects.
[after a silent moment]

I was saying, dear audience that, I don't go into good people's lives. In contrary, if you go to what you call perverted persons who practice magic art, witchcraft and other similar things that

51

you call occult sciences, you will notice that those people always consult me, unlike God who compels you to worship him without getting anything in return, except cramming those fragmented, irrelevant and complacent biblical teachings. But with me, not only they receive immediate, but positive responses to their quests. Now, who loves the humanity better than I do?

A he-advocate (2):
Wait a minute! Do you mean, you are a consultant in evil practices or what exactly are you trying to say?

Satan:
Truly speaking, I am a consultant, and people who come to my practice are my companions. Unfortunately you will realize that those people you call perverted are those who make the majority in the world.

The same he-advocate (2):
You have the magnetism of bewitching people only, and …

Satan:
[*Becoming furious and shouting*] You, human beings go to cemeteries in search of domineering powers that malicious spirits supply to all of you. There are no single good people among you. All, you are bad and hypocrite. You like money more than anything else; you envy husbands and wives of neighbors. All those acts are condemned by the Bible, but you perform them on a daily basis, you. You do have your conscience to stop you, but you refuse to use it. You perform deeds but never do you want to bear the consequences; and suddenly, when all that backfires, you accuse the devil__me. That's not right. No, ladies and gentlemen; you have no right to accuse me. Dear human beings I am not guilty. I am innocent and I should be acquitted right now.

Public Prosecutor:
Honorable President, Mr. Advocates and respectable audience, here is an illustration of an intellectual masturbation [*pointing at him*]. Honorable president, the defendant is rejoicing himself in lying and accusing us while trying to pull the curtain on his side. Wake up! [*He leaves his desk and starts addressing the audience and everybody in the court as modern priests use to do when preaching. He holds the Bible in one hand*] Wake up, fellow priests, pastors, God's children, worshippers and even new converts.

The audience:
Amen! Alleluia!

Public Prosecutor:
Praise the Lord. The devil is trying to prove us that he is Lucifer, the angel of light that he used to be, but whom he is no longer.

The audience:
Amen! Alleluia!

Public Prosecutor:
All the glory is to the Most High. Satan is the only one who is trying to persuade us that he still is the beloved arch-angel that God used to cherish. Watch out, dear brothers and sisters. We should not pay heed to his words. We should shape the iron when it is still hot.

The audience:
[*Singing*] Amen! Amen, amen, amen, amen (2x)

Public Prosecutor:
Satan appears to some people and some places, like in the city of Lourdes, in Italy, in Spain, in Philippines and some other unnamed places as the angel of light, but it is him, Satan, who disguises himself like that. Anyone who has believed in those

false appearances has been misled by this evil spirit. [*Pointing at Satan*]

The audience:
Give thanks and praises to the Lord.

Public Prosecutor:
Sure, glory to him. And we will be alright. Brothers and sisters; together in this court hall, let us resist. Such evil manifestations should not occur. The angel of light is no longer him [*pointing at him*]. He is Satan, the devil. [*A long pause*] Let's quote, brothers and sisters, 2 Corinthians 11-14 to 15 [*opening the Bible*]. Here we go. *"And no wonder, for Satan himself masquerades as an angel of light."* The holy book continues; dear brothers and sisters. *"It is not surprising, then, if his servants masquerade as servants of righteousness, their end will be what their actions deserve."*

End of quotation. Alleluia!

Satan:
Dear advocates, for clarity sake, I request that Mr. Public prosecutor answers my following question. Sir, public prosecutor…

Public Prosecutor:
Yes…

Satan:
Mr. Officer, apart from me, do you know of any other angel of light?

Public Prosecutor:
Mr. President, we know that there once was a fallen angel of light, it's him. [*Pointing at him*]

Satan:
Once more, I protest, I protest, Mr....

First Assessor:
Defendant, Lucifer the devil;

Satan:
Sir,

First Assessor:
Defendant Lucifer the devil; calm, please cool down. This court, once more reminds you that you have no right to ask any questions, but to answer our questions. You have no right to degrade anybody here. Well, proceed now!

Satan:
How come? How can I strengthen my speech without asking a question on things which are obscure to me? I mean, million accusations that you heap on me should just be swallowed without questioning their *raison d'être*? I am not a believer, but a thinker; a rational animal.

Judge President:
[*Standing up*] A piece of advice from me, Mr. Satan the devil. Forget that this court is against you. Remember, we will stick to our sacred principle of impartiality. Given our human emotion as you previously put it. In principle, we remain neutral but rejects all unfounded accusations till the end of the hearing. In simple terms, it means, the court seats not to condemn, but to make justice and if possible to acquit the innocent one. Please, compose yourself, Mr. Satan. Let us smoothly resume our trial. Defendant, Satan the devil...

Satan:
Yes, honorable president.

Judge President:
Suppose that we believe in your version of facts that you have rendered in this court. In exchange, what guarantee you do offer in order to admit that you are Lucifer, the angel of light?

Satan:
Mr. President, I do not have absolute guarantee to give you. Only, I can bring to your cognizance some elements of appreciation which would be much hazardous on your side and I am afraid, you may take them as unpredictable facts because they are related to my double personality.

First Assessor:
How come?

Satan:
Look, when I was the arch-angel Lucifer, I used to live in paradise; when I became Satan the devil by the will of human beings who misled God, the angel that I was, was "chased" from the so-called paradise. Dear human beings, "chased from paradise" is the only version of facts that you know of. But, not really what happened in there. In reality, it was a transfer from one position to another! I was just relegated to earth on a special mission for his Majesty God; that is why, very often I return to paradise to submit my report to God without your knowledge. To support my statement, I refer you on that issue, to the book of Job 1:1-12. Well, anyone may read, and I will tell you what it is all about?

Second Assessor:
I am quoting from the bible.

"In the land of Uz there lived a man whose name was Job… One day the angels came to present themselves before the Lord, and Satan also came with them. The Lord said to Satan, "Where have you come from? "Satan answered the Lord, "From the roaming through the earth and going to and from in it."

Satan:
Ah! Ah! Ah! [*Laughing*]. That's it, that's the climax; that's ultra important, dear audience. Now, you see; that one day the sons of God were reporting to him, and Satan, me__was also amongst them! Who now tells you that I never meet God? Who? We do meet, very often. Enemies in day time, friends at night. We chat quite often.

First Assessor:
Satan the devil, you do not have the floor.

Satan:
Well, Sir, I am sorry. Only that, statement of truth causes excitement. One can't resist.

First Assessor:
Please, proceed. [*To the Second Assessor*]

Second Assessor:
[*Continuing the reading*]. "*Then Satan went out from the presence of the Lord*".
End of quotation. Alleluia!

Satan:
[*Laughing*]: Look, you forget to mention that; about his servant Job, God gave me everything that belonged to him, in saying "... *everything he has is in your hand but on the man himself, do not lay a finger.*"

You see dear audience, from the reading of that passage, one can notice that God has authorized me to play my role in order to tempt the faith of Job and then, I should come to report to him. Respectable audience, in chapter 6, in the same farcical book, it is said that

"One day the angels came to present themselves before the Lord, and Satan also came with them."

End of quotation,

But, august audience, everything is crystal clear! Where could I, me *"Satan"* get the right to be amongst the angels if I was not one? Tell me!

Second Assessor:
Who knows? You could have been a spy or a blackmailer, or something like that.

Satan:
Listen to that; listen to that rubbish he is dishing out. I think I was there because of my dual personality. In addition, concerning my dual personality, august audience, I should reveal to you that, I am not the only one to hold such confusing identity. It is God's methodology. Even Jesus Christ himself has got a dubious identity! Look, about Christ, Catholics, and all other Christian related religions pretend that, Jesus is God himself. Jehovah witnesses pretend that Christ is the second person in God. Hence, the smoky theory of Trinity that has plunged the whole humanity in abominable miscomprehension. Finally, others allege that, Jesus is just a prophet like Mohammed, Buda, Kimbangu and Krishna.

Second Assessor:
So, by evoking all those examples, where do you actually want to drive us to?

Satan:
Where? Honorable audience men, those evidences lead me to the following revelation: Jesus and me are characters of the same nature. Both, we are not perfect but, are God's servants. Besides, it is by that evidence that in the Bible I am referred to as Prince

of Evil or of darkness and not King. On the other hand, Jesus is known as, Prince of peace. The king of all creation, I am saying "all" [*insisting*], is God himself. Jesus is "Prince". I am another "Prince". We share the same title as namesake!

Judge President:
Defendant Satan, the devil, things seem to go in your favour now. However, this court is still awaiting convincing arguments that can help us to acquit you.

Satan:
I understand your impatience Mr. President. Pretty soon, you'll be served.

Judge President:
I am warning, Mr. Satan, sorry, Mr. Devil, sorry again, Mr. Lucifer; the triviality of your discourse may work against you. Do you measure the impact of the desolation that you are inflicting on the Christian community by questioning even the holiness of Christ? If you were a Christian, you'd be excommunicated right on the spot.

Satan:
I would not care, Mr. President. It's the least of my pre-occupations. Because, both Jesus and his so-called father need me. But, I don't need them at all. I am independent. Both consult me in whatever aim to achieve.

[*A long silence in the court*]

Judge President:
How is it possible that both you and Jesus Christ can share the same spiritual nature, yet the purposes of your existence diverge? You are complaining that the Public Prosecutor does not respect the law, which for the present moment is Bible-based in this era.

But, you, which legal texts do you refer to, to claim that Jesus Christ was not perfect?

Satan:
Mr. President, I don't need any text to refer to; nevertheless learn that Jesus Christ is the product of two seeds: one pure and another impure; in other words, Jesus was born of God, as they teach you; God, the absolute perfection [*ironising*] and of Mary, the imperfection per excellence, because, she is of human race. Well, biologically, Jesus would have been a hybrid child who would have…

Public Prosecutor:
Stop [*to Satan*]. Your Honour,[*to the Judge President*] Mary was found holy by God, which is why the fruit of the conception is also holy.

Satan:
Ah! I see, Mr. Officer. What about the rest of other women on the earth. You want to say there is no saint among them? The yellow, the blacks, etc…, all of them are witches, bitches? And why Mary should continue to be called "virgin" even after giving birth to more than one child? Besides what is virgin in her?

Public Prosecutor:
[*After starring at him*] Madness! Well, in the book of Luke 1:35, we learn that;

"The Holy Spirit will come upon you, and the power of the Most High will overshadow you. So the holy one to be born will be called the son of God."

End of quotation.

Your honour, [*to the Judge President*] if by analogy, the son who will be born will be holy, we can conclude that prior to the conception, the mother must have been sanctified before; even if that is not written in the Bible.

Satan:
No, no, no. No! This is a statement of authority.

Public Prosecutor:
Yes, otherwise, the child who would be born would not be holy!

Satan:
No, your worship. No, no, no, that's a bad interpretation, Mr. Prosecutor. Mr.Officer, the word of God is a testament as you human beings continue to assert it. And if such is the case, it is known universally that the law insists on the authenticity of a will. The law recommends that a will should remain intact; I mean, it should not suffer any alterations. I know that, you are a so-called minister of God. Thus, given that competence, you have no right to alter anything; but God has.

Someone from the audience (B):
And God is not dead yet. He is ever living. Satan, pay attention, ministers of God are always inspired, sir. It is not amazing if the public prosecutor is under spiritual visions. That's why you fail to comprehend his language and the extent to which he is leading you, sir.

Public Prosecutor:
Do you get that? God is now talking through his real children. Not yo...

Satan:
Garbage [*dismissing it with his hand*] Mr. Officer. You are not the author of the Bible to empower yourself and say what the Bible has understated. You can't neither interpret nor misinterpret that book you are holding. No, no, no, no. If ever you dare do it, it

means you are a merchant of charm and a perfect seducer. You are a spiritual businessman who is also leading people astray to make money out of them.

Public Prosecutor:
Your Honour, the word of God is an exceptional testament. By testament of exception, I mean a well-inspired book which has no mistakes. Somewhere in the Bible, it is said that, Jesus Christ will come back to tie up the devil; and, this man knows that he has shorter time on this earth before he got arrested and thrown into jail for eternity. Mr. President, Mr. Satan is trying to disturb us in order to win the case, because, whosoever says the truth does not need to talk too much in order to prove his innocence. Such a step is one of the characteristics of a liar.

Satan:
[*After a long silence*]: This comedy has lasted long and I want to do away with it once and for all. I am now pretty bored with this shit.

First Assessor:
Defendant Satan the devil.

Satan:
Sir,...

First Assessor:
Defendant Lucifer the devil, a bit of modesty in your language, please. It is not a comedy here as you allege, but you are on trial. And, it's ultra serious. Please, withdraw your words.

Satan:
As you like it, I withdraw them; but I do not reject them.

First Assessor:
Thanks. Let's proceed.

Satan:

[*Now furious*] Mr. President, I was saying, I can't bear your comedy any longer. What I want to tell you is the plain truth and you can take it or leave it if you want. Then do whatever you want with me at last, if ever you can, you creatures with small mind. I don't beg anything.

Second Assessor:

[*Interrupting abruptly and talking to the audience*]: This is an insult to us as human beings. Ladies and gentlemen, I sense it, there gonna be fireworks in the air right now. It is intolerable.

The audience:

[*shouting*]Blast it, blast it, blast it up, fireworks...

Judge President:

Silence [*angered & hammering the table*]. Silence, I said. I am reminding you that we are in a court, not a religious revival gathering. Stop shaming our human nature in front of this visitor; stop being hilarious and agitated in here. Police officers, I order you to post yourselves one by one in each raw and monitor that instinctive eruption of human nature that's trying to dent our dignity in here. [*Turning to Satan*] I am sorry, Mr. Lucifer. It was worthy it. The floor is yours.

Satan:

Thanks, your Excellency. Listen, dear human beings. This trial is an illustration of your vanity, your arrogance and ignorance of the origin of creation. Do you really think, by trying me, you are making justice or are defending the interests of God? You allege that your God instructs you to fight me, to chase me, and perhaps to kill me. This is ridiculous and ludicrous. But how come? Since creation, the same God has never fought me, chased me nor killed me? Hein! Much wrong has been done on earth ever since your existence, you, human race. And, the daily allegation is always that, the cause is me, the devil?

Second Assessor:
Your honour, please, stop this bandit from delusion.

Judge President:
Give him a chance. No stone should remain unturned today. Defendant Satan, please, carry on.

Satan:
Thanks, Mr. President. I was talking about God; him who is omnipotent, omnipresent and so forth and so on. Have you ever seen that God you pray and believe in? But, me, I know him. We have been together since creation. If himself can't kill me, how can you small and incapable creatures prosecute me? If God can't judge me, who can judge me? Who gives you that right and power to try a partner of your creator who participated in your molding? Are you paranoiac?

First Assessor:
Mr. Satan, do you mean God has hidden something from us? That, we are ignorant of; and...

Satan:
Not only ignorant sir, but you are too small to transcend the natural mystery. There are lots of things that God has hidden from you and will never reveal to you as the Bible says it in Matthew 15:26 *"It is not right to take the children's bread and toss it to the dogs"*.

Someone from the audience (C):
You mean, us human beings are "dogs"?

Satan:

I am not the one who says so! Rather, it is your "Holy Book"; the one you pretend bears no mistake nor abusive language which says it.

Someone from the audience (C):

You really do not understand in what context Jesus Christ said that.

Satan:

You call him what? "Christ"? But, even himself refused to be called by that name! Read Matthew 16:20 where he warned his disciples *"Do not tell anyone that I am the Christ."*

Public Prosecutor:

Mr. President, Satan says that we have never seen God? He must be sick of such a dangerous declaration. But, the whole nature we're living in is a living manifestation of God: the sun, moon, ocean, mountains, valleys and beautiful forests are all physical presence of God. Can he explain to us where did all these items come from? There should be a maker for all this...

Satan:

Which nature are you talking about? The one you are destroying? Ungrateful creatures. You are killing this Mother Nature everyday with your pollution and negligence! This nature which feeds you, protects you and thanks to which you are living?

Someone from the audience (A):

It's finished with you today. We will deal with you; intriguing character.

Satan:

Your rotten comedy must now end. Your intelligence is limited and you pretend to know more than I do. Imbeciles, hypocrites. You visit fortune-tellers, you go practice occult sciences in order to strengthen your power and dominate others, you open churches to mislead others in order to make money and break marriages of your neighbors. You kill because of jealousy and selfishness. You crafted economic and political systems such as Capitalism, Communism, Apartheid, racism, colonialism and imperialism in order to enslave your brother men and take advantage of them.

Judge President:
Mr. Satan, stop, stop it…

Satan:
Now, you coin a new system called "Globalization" in order to pillage and plunder the resources of virgin countries under the guise of developing them. Gosh, all those evils do not come from me! They are the result of your consciousness. Because God has given you the free choice to do good or wrong. If God was love, how could he tempt you by putting in front of you those two options? Making the evil more attractive than the goodness.

Judge President:
Defendant Satan, I said, stop.

Public Prosecutor:
You're a crazy dog [*to Satan*]. If the President says stop, you must obey. This is a human court. Not hell court where you can rule as you like.

Satan:
I need no instruction from a misleading person like you. You capitalize on the Bible to produce money for your personal gains. It is me who should be doing that job which you now have hijacked. Liar; lazy imposter.

First Assessor:

[*Rising up*]: Silence, silence in the court. You don't realize to which extent you hurt His Majesty God with awkward statements in this court. Mr. Public prosecutor, Mr. Satan, you need to reconcile now before we smoothly proceed with the hearing.

Satan:

I cannot reconcile with a merchant of lie; let me continue from where I stopped. Dear naïve human beings; how can you claim that God loves you? And, as you always do wrong; where is my responsibility in all that? You hijack all the powers in the world by saying; God is male, all the angels are males, Jesus male, all the disciples of Jesus, males, most of saints, males; and nothing for women? Is it still me who impose such gender divide in your midst? Women have become endangered species on earth, because of you. Selfish creatures.

Public Prosecutor:

Many a time, I have told you that God never tempts anyone.

Satan:

Don't rewind the tape of your nonsense here, my dear. You are making a grievous mistake by putting and chaining me in this box; a celestial being that I am. I refer you to the Bible. Read Jude 8 to 10. Read it, read it now.

Public Prosecutor:

May I, may I… [*Asking permission from the court president*]

Judge President:

Oh! Sure! Satan the devil, what was the reference as you said?

Satan:

Mr. President, I said, Jude 8 to 10. [*To the audience*] Be attentive. You'll get the recipe of your life.

Public Prosecutor:
[*After opening the Bible*] *"In the very same, these dreamers pollute their own bodies, reject authority and slander celestial beings. But even the arch angel Michael when he was disputing with the devil about the body of Moses, did not dare to bring a slanderous accusation against him, but said, "The Lord rebukes you!" Yet these men speak abusively against whatever they do not understand; and what things they do understand by instinct, like unreasoning animals__these are the very things that destroy them."* [*He remains silent, and then starts shaking. The Bible falls down. Then after, he picks it up*]

Satan:
You see, you see now? What did I tell you? If creatures of heaven can respect me as the Bible says, how can you mammals with no intelligence dare disrespect me? When I was disputing the body of Moses in the heavens, the angel never insulted me, nor accused me of any wrongdoing! Because I am superior to all creatures.

Judge President:
Mr. Public prosecutor.

Public Prosecutor:
Your worship.

Judge President:
Do you still have anything to say against the defendant?

Public Prosecutor:
Understand that God has promised to send Christ to take those who have believed in him and bring them to heavens and next, he will destroy all non believers and all who dwell on this earth. He, [*pointing at Satan*] will be among them. He won't survive this time. Refer to Revelation 20:1-3.

Satan:

Bull shit! You didn't finish the reading of the third paragraph. The book of Revelation on that verse concludes that: *"After that, he must be set free for a short time."* [*He starts laughing*]. Poor human beings, you can't understand the agreement between me and God. It's a mystery for nonentities like you. You can't live thousands years, but me, I can. Read it in the Revelation 20:1-3.

Public Prosecutor:

[*Laughing too*] You have no chance to escape from the judgment day. Read it in Revelation 20:7 to 10. Mr. President, owing to the length of this passage, allow me to read for you, the audience and defendant, only the tenth verse.

Judge President:

Please, do.

Public Prosecutor:

"And the devil, who deceived them, was thrown into the lake of burning sulfur, where the beast and the false prophet had been thrown. They will be tormented day and night for ever and ever."

End of quotation.
Alleluia. Praises and glory to the Lord.

Satan:

[*Laughing loudly and longingly*] People of small minds, you know nothing about my doom. There is no doom's day for me. The Bible says, we will "suffer"; we will be "tormented"; of course, but not dead! I am used to suffering. But you will disappear for good. I don't die! And, Mr. President and respectable audience, I still refer you to the book of Samuel 16:14 and Samuel 18:10. Mr. Prosecutor, read it.

Public Prosecutor:
This time no. Not me. Somebody else. It is just getting above my nerves.

Judge President:
[*To the Second Assessor*] Could you please, read those passages?

Second Assessor:
[*Asking for the Bible from the P.P*]: May I get it, sir?

Public Prosecutor:
Here you go.

Second Assessor:
"Now the spirit of the Lord had departed from Saul, and an evil spirit from the Lord tormented him." That was Samuel 18:14. Now let me read from the same book, on 18:10. It says: *"The next day an evil spirit from God came forcefully upon Saul."*

[*The P.P and the panel of judges seem to be agitated as they start looking up and down, left and right, not knowing what to do and to say.*]

Satan:
Look at that, gentlemen! How can a Holy God, with pure spirit send simultaneously a bad and a holy spirit? That's controversial! You call such a manual a Holy Book? You still insist that God is perfect? Dear brothers and sisters in ignorance and fear; look at what I lastly have to advise you as you believe in the righteousness of your God: pray really and always do good. Who knows? Your salvation may come out of that!

Judge President:
[*Standing up*] Dear public prosecutor, distinguished members of the jury and the respectable audience whose patience and attention have helped to smoothly continue with the hearings; this court

asks for your permission to consult its members in camera after which we will announce the verdict. Thank you. [*The jury withdraws and goes behind wall. The devil remains there, with his body guard.*]

Noise from the audience:
You will see. It's over with you today. The deceiver of humanity, the accuser, the blackmailer, power usurper, thief, killer, poisonous creature, you'll be nailed today. Schizophrenic, alcoholic, paranoiac, myth maniac and blunderer.

[*They start hurling missiles at him; police officers who were standing up try to diffuse the crisis when the jury returns into the hall.*]

Police officers:
Silence, silence, silence in the court. [*The audience stands up as the court president enters the last.*]

Judge President:
Thank you. Please, regain your seats. Dear judges, august audience. This court, facing an unusual case since the establishment of human kind's justice system; having had no evidence on the guiltiness of the defendant, Mr. Satan; this court, ladies and gentlemen was I saying, is incapacitated to indict Mr. Lucifer on false allegations leveled upon him. On the benefit of doubt, as there is no proof of his wrong doing since men have been given the free choice by God: to do evil or good; yet, man, being the likeness of God but prefers to do wrong and escapes from assuming the responsibilities of his deeds by finding scapegoats. In order to maintain the legendary impartiality of our justice system, as we all believe in God, the Most High and father of universe; this court said I, solemnly acquits Mr. Lucifer and sets him free from now on. This court condemns man of rebellion against God. The Bible says *"resist him and he will flee from you. God gave you the power through the Holy Spirit to step on the devil."* [*Turning his head to Satan*] Mr. Lucifer, you are acquitted, and now, can walk

71

out of this court as a free man in order to pursue your mission as assigned by God himself.

Satan:
Thanks, Mr. President. However, I would like to rectify one thing. [*The president looks amazed*]

Judge President:
Yes, which one?

Satan:
I am not a "man" as you say. I and God are the same. The Holy Ghost does not exist. It is a fabrication of some religious societies. They are associations of evil-doers. Call me Lucifer, the light-bearer angel. For ever and ever.

Public Prosecutor:
And Jesus?

Satan:
He is as a human being as you are. Which man can save his brother's soul? Remember, it's just self-control. He is a Prince, I am another Prince. He died for usurping the power of others and the whole world can't be held responsible for his death; if at all he died.

Judge President [*after a long stare*]:
Mr. Satan, you are acquitted. [*The jury stands up*]

The audience:
Traitors, traitors, traitors, corrupt magistrates, useless justice, fearful magistrates, we will kill you, kill them, burn them, shoot them etc...

Satan:
Small heads! [*To the crowd*]

[*Trouble starts in the hall as human beings hurl missiles onto the devil and the jury. Hurly-burly ensues. The devil blows the whistle he was wearing around his neck and strange creatures land in the hall, fighting men.*]

The End.

Glossary

Dunia Yetu: Our world [Swahili]

Grande première: the first of its kind [French]

Pro-tempore: for the moment [Latin]

En-passant: in passing, [French]

Eli, Eli, Lama sabachani: God, God, why have you forsaken me

Raison d'être: Raison for being [French]

About the author

Jemadari Vi-Bee-Kil Kilele is the author of:

- ❖ **The Afrikan Tales;** a collection of short stories.
- ❖ **The Serial Killer,** a play.
- ❖ **The Private Secretary,** a play.
- ❖ **Alien,** a play.

The Trial of Satan is his fourth play; and now he is working towards his first novels: **A Season of Vultures** and **2010.**

As a poet, he recently has released volumes of poetry in both French and English.

- ❖ **Spleen;** and
- ❖ **La Bille Echauffee**

Jemadari is a well-known and renowned Educationist, whom since 1991 founded and has been managing the **Sheikh Anta Diop College** in Johannesburg, South Africa.

He is a political activist too.